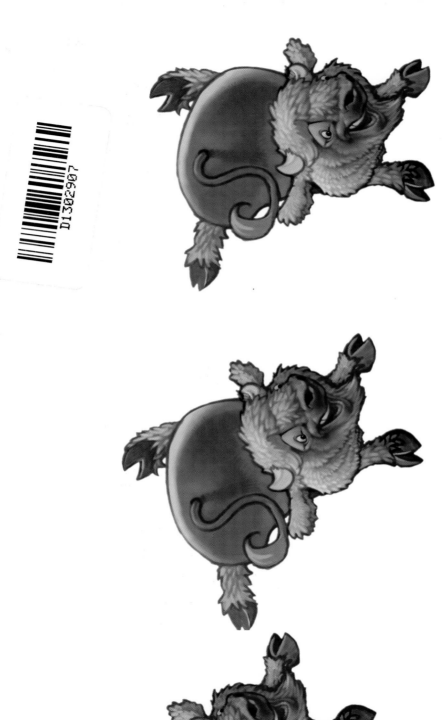

Don't Tell That to Beasley

by Tara McClary Reeves &
Christa McClary McElveen

Illustrated by Justin Gerard of Portland Studios

WATERBROOK
PRESS

DON'T TELL THAT TO BEASLEY

PUBLISHED BY WATERBROOK PRESS
2375 Telstar Drive, Suite 160
Colorado Springs, Colorado 80920
A division of Random House, Inc.

ISBN 1-57856-982-6

Copyright © 2005 by Tara M. Reeves

Library of Congress Cataloging-in-Publication Data
Reeves, Tara McClary.
Don't tell that to Beasley / by Tara McClary Reeves and Christa McClary McElveen ; illustrated by Justin Gerard.— 1st ed.
    p. cm.
Summary: Beasley the buffalo likes doing things that other buffaloes do not like to do, from playing football and picking flowers to eating marshmallows and brushing his teeth.
    ISBN 1-57856-982-6
    [1. Bison—Fiction. 2. Individuality—Fiction.] I. Title: Do not tell that to Beasley. II. McElveen, Christa McClary. III. Gerard, Justin, ill. IV. Title.
    PZ7.R2584Don 2005
    [E]—dc22

2005005044

Printed in Mexico
2005—First Edition

10 9 8 7 6 5 4 3 2 1

With love to our husbands,
Lee Reeves and John McElveen;
and to our children,
Caroline and Daniel, John Thomas and Madeline

Buffalo aren't supposed to like milkshakes.

But don't tell that to Beasley!

Buffalo aren't supposed to like playing hide-and-seek.

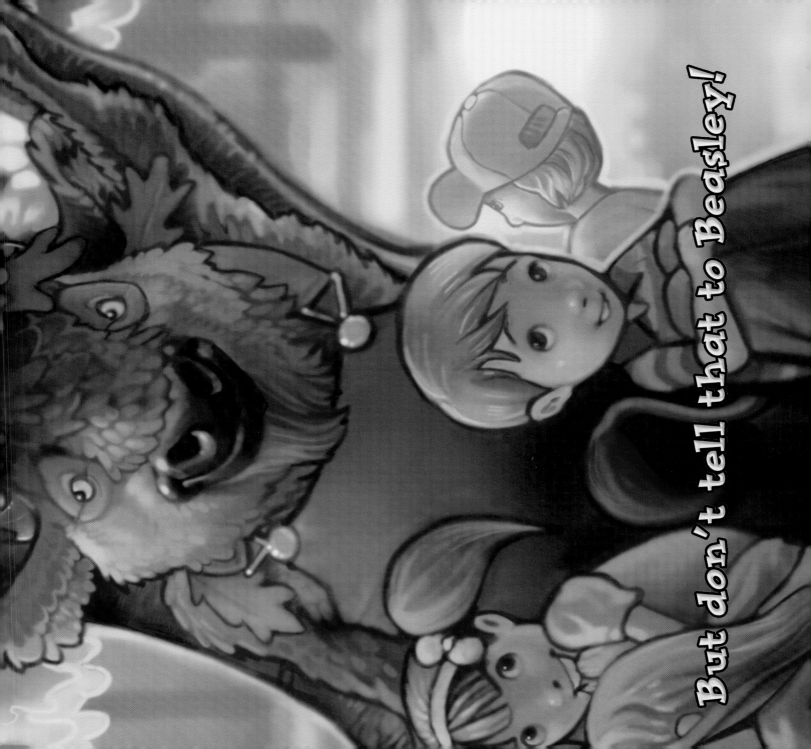

Buffalo aren't supposed to like taking baths.

But don't tell that to Beasley!

Buffalo aren't supposed to like playing make-believe.

But don't tell that to Beasley!

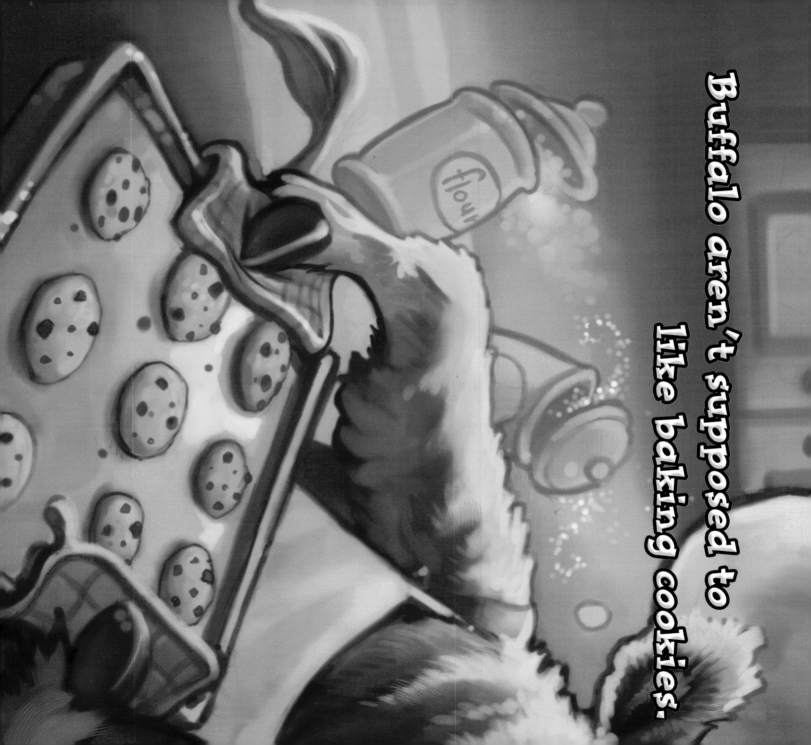

Buffalo aren't supposed to like baking cookies.

Buffalo aren't supposed to like cleaning their rooms.

Buffalo aren't supposed to like singing and dancing.

But don't tell that to Beasley!

Buffalo aren't supposed to like playing football.

But don't tell that to Beasley!

Buffalo aren't supposed to like picking flowers.

But don't tell that to Beasley!

Buffalo aren't supposed to like playing at the beach.

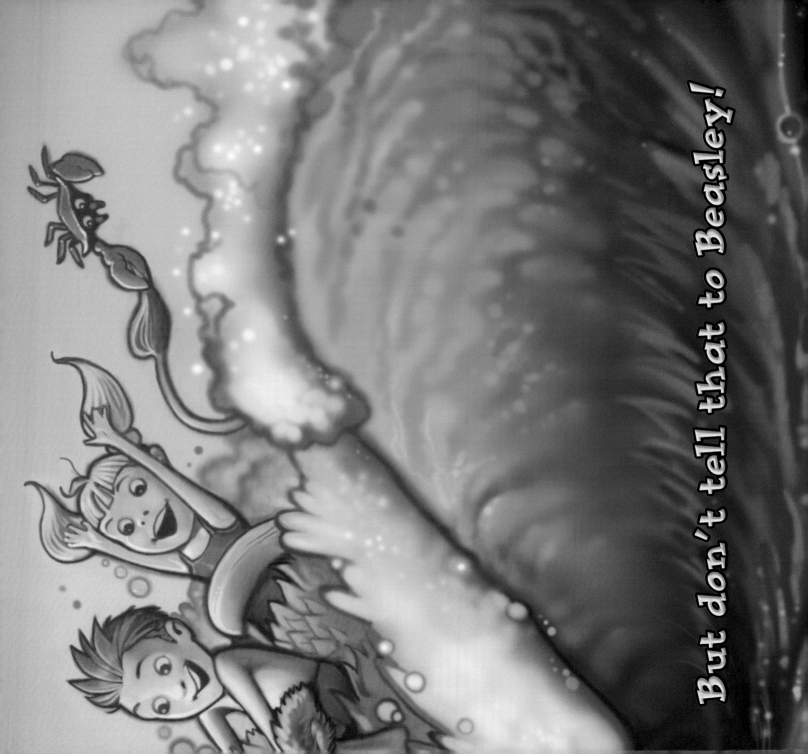

But don't tell that to Beasley!

Buffalo aren't supposed to like brushing their teeth.

But don't tell that to Beasley!

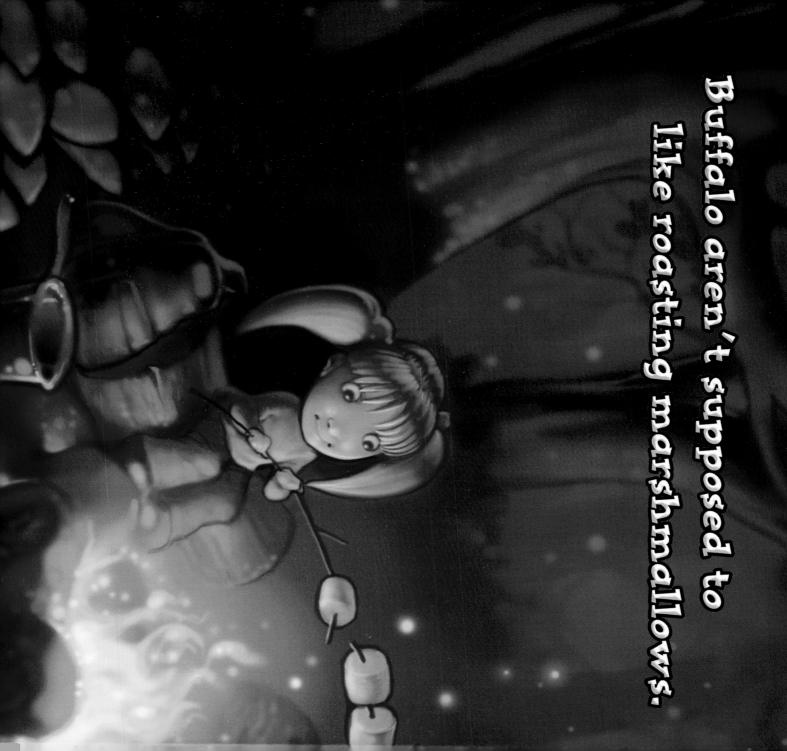

Buffalo aren't supposed to like roasting marshmallows.

But don't tell that to Beasley!

Buffalo aren't supposed to like reading books.

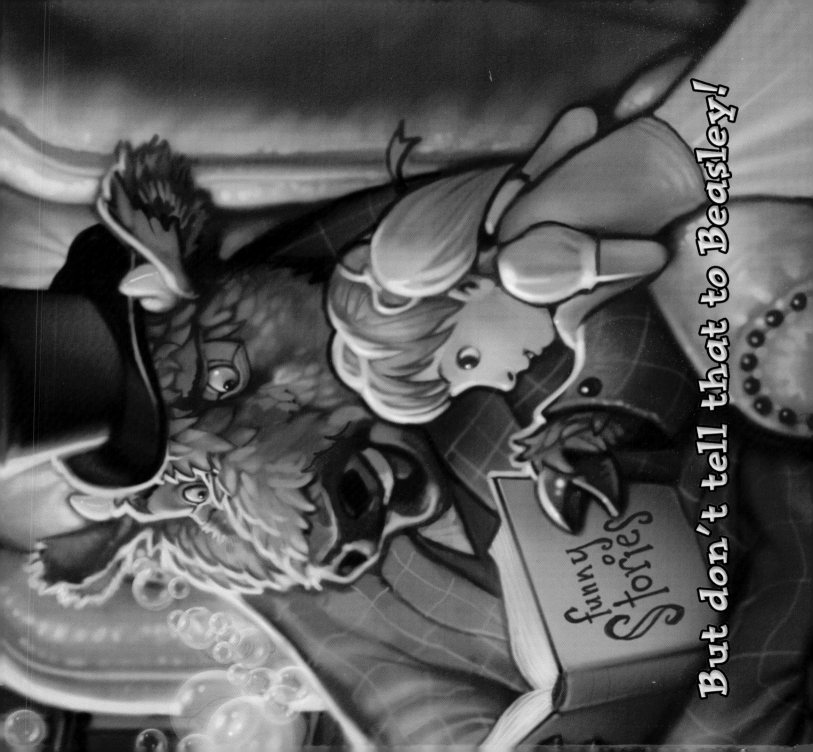

But don't tell that to Beasley!

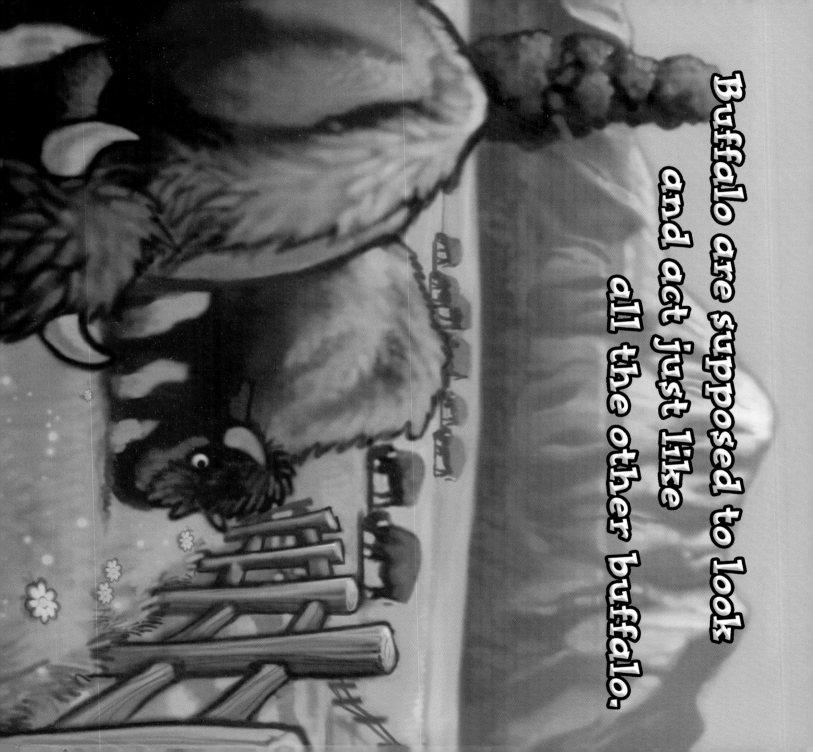

Buffalo are supposed to look and act just like all the other buffalo.

But don't tell that to Beasley!